Susan Arkin Couture

THE BLOCK BOOK

illustrated by

Petra Mathers

HARPER & ROW, PUBLISHERS

Betsy and Ben

were industrious blocks.

They made their own cocoa

and washed their own socks.

They lived in a tower

they'd built by themselves,

with turrets and tunnels

and doorways and shelves.

Betsy and Ben

had a great many things:

umbrellas and yo-yos,

old sneakers and springs,

an old, rusty clock

and a worn-out beret.

They just couldn't bear

to throw good junk away.

Their house got so crowded;

they slept in the yard

on old magazines and

a Valentine's card.

Till one day a neighbor,

one J. Beeswax Brown

came calling,

"Please help me,

my house just burnt down.

"If you have some old bits
of junk you can spare,
I'll build a new house
on that hill over there."

"Have we got some junk,

are you kidding?" they cried.

"Come in, have a look—shove

that bass drum aside!"

They loaded the truck

and went speeding away.

They hammered and stacked

and cemented all day,

till there stood a "Whosis,"

a house but not quite.

Whatever it was—

a beautiful sight!

"It's time to go home,"
Betsy said with a yawn,
while stooping to pick up
some cans on the lawn.

"I'm ready," said Ben,
as he picked up a spoon,
three keys, a dried leaf,
and a drifting balloon.

They didn't get home
until midnight, I think.
The last thing they found
was an old kitchen sink.

"Oh well," chuckled Betsy,
"we've done it again."
"There's more where that
came from—tomorrow," said Ben.

For Kaelin and Lauren
S. A. C.
meinen geliebten Eltern
P. M.

The Block Book
Text copyright © 1990 by Susan Birkenhead
Illustrations copyright © 1990 by Petra Mathers
Printed in the U.S.A. All rights reserved.
Typography by Andrew Rhodes
1 2 3 4 5 6 7 8 9 10
First Edition

Library of Congress Cataloging-in-Publication Data
Couture, Susan Arkin.
  The block book / Susan Arkin Couture ; illustrated by Petra
Mathers.
     p.   cm.
  Summary: Betsy and Ben, two industrious blocks who love to
collect junk, use their junk to help a friend in need.
  ISBN 0-06-020523-7 : $. — ISBN 0-06-020524-5 (lib. bdg.):
$
  [1. Blocks (Toys)—Fiction.   2. Stories in rhyme.] I. Mathers,
Petra, ill. II. Title
PZ8.3.C8335B1   1990   89-34504
[F]—dc90   CIP
                                                        AC